THE KING'S DRUM

by the same author

The King's Drum
and Other African Stories

Harold Courlander
Illustrated by Enrico Arno

Harcourt, Brace & World, Inc., New York

Contents

THE KING'S DRUM

The Song of Gimmile

Gindo Tribe, Mali

ONCE there was Konondjong, a great King of the Gindo people.

One day a singer from Korro came to Bankassi, where Konondjong lived. He went to the King's house and sang for him. He played on his lute and sang about famous warriors and their deeds, about things that had happened in the world, and about the accomplishments of the chiefs of former times. King Konondjong was entertained by what he heard. When the singing was finished, Konondjong asked the singer what he wanted in Bankassi. The bard replied: "Oh, sir, all I want is a small gift from you."

The King said in surprise: "You ask the King of the Gindo people for a gift?"

"Only a small gift, a token in exchange for my singing," the bard answered.

"Ah!" Konondjong said with exasperation. "Here is a homeless bard who presumes to ask the King of the Gindo for a present! Many famous bards come and sing for the honor of being heard, but this man asks for something in return! Whoever gave me such disrespect before? Take him away and give him fifty lashes."

So King Konondjong's servants took the bard and beat
him with a knotted rope for punishment. The singer then
made his way home to Korro.

In Korro there lived a man by the name of Gimmile.
Gimmile heard the story of what happened to the bard
who sang for King Konondjong. So he composed a song
of contempt about the king. It went:

> "Konondjong, King of the Gindo,
>   He is fat, his neck is flabby.
>   Konondjong, King of the Gindo,
>   His teeth are few, his legs are swelled.
>   Konondjong, King of the Gindo,
>   His knees are bony, his head is bald.
>   Konondjong, King of the Gindo."

This was the song made by Gimmile. He went out
where the people were, taking his harp with him, and he
sang his song. Gimmile's voice was good. The music of
his song was catching. Soon other people of Korro were
singing this song. It became popular among the people
and the bards. Travelers who came to Korro took the song
away and sang it elsewhere. It was heard at dances and
festivals. Among the Gindo people it was known everywhere.

> "Konondjong, King of the Gindo,
>   He is fat, his neck is flabby.
>   Konondjong, King of the Gindo,
>   His teeth are few, his legs are swelled.
>   Konondjong, King of the Gindo,
>   His knees are bony, his head is bald.
>   Konondjong, King of the Gindo."

Women sang it while grinding corn. Girls sang it while

carrying water. Men sang it while working in the fields.

King Konondjong heard the people singing it. He was angered. He asked: "Who has made this song?"

And the people replied: "It was made by a singer in Korro."

Konondjong sent messengers to Korro to the bard whom he had mistreated. The bard came to Bankassi, and the King asked him: "Who is the maker of this song?"

The bard replied: "It was made by Gimmile of Korro."

The King gave the bard a present of one hundred thousand cowry shells, a horse, a cow, and an ox. He said: "See to it that Gimmile's song is sung no more."

The bard said: "Oh, sir, I was whipped with a knotted rope when I sang for you. Even though you are a king, you cannot retract it. A thing that is done cannot be undone. A song that is not composed does not exist; but once it is made, it is a real thing. Who can stop a song that travels from country to country? All of the Gindo people sing it. I am not the King. If the great King of the Gindo cannot prevent the song of Gimmile from being sung, my power over the people is certainly less."

The song of Gimmile was sung among the people, and it is preserved to this day, for King Konondjong could not bring it to an end.

The King was not compelled to beat the bard, but he did, and then it could not be undone.

Gimmile did not have to make a song about the King, but he did, and it could not be stopped.

The Chief of the Gurensi

Gurensi Tribe, Upper Volta and Ghana

T is said that one time the Chief of the Gurensi people had to make a long journey to the south, but he was concerned about the welfare of his daughter during his absence. He went to his friend named Money and said to him, "I shall be gone one month, two months—who knows how long? Watch my daughter for me while I am gone. If men come with the hope of marrying her, turn them away; I will speak with them when I return."

Money replied, "Yes, do not worry; I will see after her."

The Chief went on his journey. One month, two months passed, and he did not return. Men came to ask about the Chief's daughter. They wished to marry her. But Money turned them away. When the Chief had been gone many months, Money said, "Something has happened to my friend the Chief. He is not coming home."

A young man came to ask for the Chief's daughter. Money said, "Her father went away and never returned. He put her in my charge. So you must make the marriage settlement with me."

The young man and Money discussed the marriage settlement. They argued. At last they settled the amount.

The young man brought many cowries. He brought cloth. He brought copper bars. He brought a horse. He brought many things and paid them to Money for the marriage settlement. Then the young man took the Chief's daughter and went away to another village to the north. Money said to himself, "Indeed, now I am rich."

A day came when it was said that the Chief was returning. Money said, "He told me to send the suitors away, and I did not do it. His daughter is no more in his house. I thought the Chief was dead, but now he returns. I received the marriage settlement for myself. How can I face him?"

Money took his family and everything he owned and went away. He traveled far, fearing that the Chief would come after him and bring him back. He went across the grassy plains. He disappeared from the country.

The Chief came back to his village. He came to his house, saying, "Where is my daughter?"

The people said, "Your friend Money took the marriage settlement and gave her to a suitor."

He replied, "Bring Money here at once."

They said, "It cannot be done. Money has fled out of the country."

The Chief said, "Money has broken his word. He has given my daughter away in my absence. He has taken the marriage settlement for himself. Find him. Bring him back."

They asked, "Wherever shall we look for him?"

He said, "Look everywhere. The matter cannot be closed until he is brought back."

The people looked. When they went hunting, they also sought the Chief's friend. When they met Hausa traders

from the north they asked, "Have you seen Money?" And the traders asked in every village through which they passed, "Is Money here?"

Time passed. The Chief of the Gurensi became old and died. Still the people searched. They never stopped. The son of the Chief became Chief. He grew old and died. Still the search went on.

This is why it is said that people everywhere are always looking for Money.

Three Fast Men

Mende Tribe, Ivory Coast

HREE young men went out to their fields to harvest millet. It began to rain. One of the men carried a basket of millet on his head. The earth was wet from the rain, and the man slipped. His foot skidded from the city of Bamako to the town of Kati. The basket of millet on his head began to fall. The man reached into a house as he slid by and picked up a knife. He cut the tall reed grass that grew along the path, wove a mat out of it, and laid it on the ground beneath him. Spilling from the falling basket, the millet fell upon the mat. The man arose, shook the millet from the mat back into the basket, and said: "If I had not had the presence of mind to make a mat and put it beneath me, I would have lost my grain."

The second young man had forty chickens in fifteen baskets, and on the way to his millet field he took the chickens from the baskets to let them feed. Suddenly a hawk swooped down, its talons ready to seize one of the chickens. The man ran swiftly among his chickens, picked them up, put each one in its proper basket, covered the baskets, and caught the swooping hawk by its talons. He said, "What do you think you are doing—trying to steal my chickens?"

17

The third young man and the first young man went hunting together. The first man shot an arrow at an antelope. The other man leaped forward at the same instant, caught the antelope, killed it, skinned it, cut up the meat, stretched the skin out to dry, and placed the meat in his knapsack. Then he reached out his hand and caught the first man's arrow as it arrived. He said, "What do you think you are doing—trying to shoot holes in my knapsack?"

The King of Sedo

Wolof Tribe, Senegal

N the town of Sedo, it is said, there was a King named Sabar. Sabar's armies were powerful. They conquered many towns, and many people paid tribute to him. If a neighboring Chief passed through Sedo, he came to Sabar's house, touched his forehead to the ground, and presented gifts to the King. As the King grew old, he grew proud. His word was law in Sedo. And if his word was heard in other places, it was law there too. Sabar said to himself, "I am indeed great, for who is there to contradict me? And who is my master?"

There came to Sedo one day a minstrel, and he was called on to entertain the King. He sang a song of praise to Sabar and to Sabar's ancestors. He danced. And then he sang:

> "The dog is great among dogs,
>   Yet he serves man.
>   The woman is great among women,
>   Yet she waits upon her children.
>   The hunter is great among hunters,
>   Yet he serves the village.

Minstrels are great among minstrels,
Yet they sing for the King and his slaves."

When the song was finished, Sabar said to the minstrel, "What is the meaning of this song?"

The minstrel replied, "The meaning is that all men serve, whatever their station."

And Sabar said to him, "Not all men. The King of Sedo does not serve. It is others who serve him."

The minstrel was silent, and Sabar asked, "Is this not the truth?"

The minstrel answered, "Who am I to say the King of Sedo speaks what is not true?"

At this moment a wandering holy man came through the crowd and asked for some food. The minstrel said to the King, "Allow me to give this unfortunate man a little of the food which you have not eaten."

Sabar said, "Give it, and let us get on with the discussion."

The minstrel said, "Here is my harp until I have finished feeding him." He placed his harp in the King's hands, took a little food from the King's bowl, and gave it to the holy man. Then he came back and stood before Sabar.

"O King of Sedo," he said, "you have spoken what I could not say, for who contradicts a king? You have said that all men serve the King of Sedo and that he does not serve. Yet you have given a wandering holy man food from your bowl, and you have held the harp for a mere minstrel while he served another. How then can one say a king does not serve? It is said, 'The head and the body must serve each other.'"

And the minstrel picked up his harp from the hands of the King and sang:

> "The soldier is great among soldiers,
>   Yet he serves the clan.
>   The King is great among kings,
>   Yet he serves his people."

The Fisherman

Jabo Tribe, Liberia

SEA gull, the fisherman, lived on the shore of the great ocean. Each day he waited until the tide went out, and then he found many small fish left in little pools along the water's edge.

One day the gull waited patiently for the tide to go down so that he could begin eating. But it seemed to him that the water didn't get lower at all but rose higher and higher. The gull was perplexed. "Formerly at this time of day the sea went down," he said. "Now it is coming up. I wonder what is the matter?"

He decided to consult some other people and make inquiries about the situation. So he flew to the village where the chickens lived. At the gate he met a rooster.

"One moment, my friend," the gull said. "I need your advice. When does the low tide of the ocean generally begin?"

The rooster answered, "Low tide? Just what do you mean by that? And what is this thing, ocean, that you are talking about?"

The gull had no time for explanations. He flew off, and after a while he met a duck swimming in a lake. He said,

"One moment, friend. What time does the high tide end and the low tide begin?"

"What are you talking about?" the duck answered. "There is no high tide or low tide. The water here always remains the same."

"I am speaking of the ocean," the gull said. "I don't speak of this miserable little lake."

"Ocean? Whatever is that?" the duck asked.

"What kind of people are these?" the gull said. "They know nothing at all about important things." He flew on toward the bush country and came to a flock of rice birds feeding in a field.

"Friends," he said to them, "what time does the ocean tide go out?"

"Ocean tide go out?" they answered. "We don't know about such things. We are busy getting our rice before the farmer comes to drive us away. We have no time for this kind of conversation."

So the gull flew on. He came to one village, then another, asking the same question and getting no answer. Deep in the bush country, he met a mourning dove who sat in a tree crying over and over, "Neo-o-o balo-o-o! huuu! huuu! huuu!" The gull interrupted, saying, "Excuse me, friend. What time does the sea go down?"

The mourning dove answered: "Don't you see that I am mourning the death of my mother? Why do you bother me with questions at a time like this? Go find the pigeon; he is the one that knows the time of things."

And the gull flew on. Far in the bush country he found the pigeon. He said: "People around here are not helpful. When a question is asked, they know nothing of the answer. But you, you have been highly recommended. Tell me, when does the tide of the ocean fall? This is a matter of great importance, for I eat when the low tide leaves fish in the pools along the ocean's edge."

The pigeon replied: "You live at the ocean's edge, while I live here in the bush country. Isn't it strange that you, a seacoast dweller, come to me, a bush dweller who has never seen the sea, to ask what time the tide falls? Begone, you stupid creature. Go back where you came from. The gull should not ask the pigeon about affairs of the ocean."

It is said: "Every man should be the master of his own profession."

A Song for the New Chief

Ashanti Tribe, Ghana

T is said that there was a Chief of Agona, and the people had grown accustomed to him. He ruled many years, he grew old, he died. The royal family selected another Chief to replace him. His name was Adoko.

The procession that brought him to the Chief's house was long, as long as from the town of Kibi to the town of Koforidua. Drummers marched in front of the procession, playing on their drums. What their drums said was, "Our Chief is great; Adoko is wise." In the city there was a great celebration. Musicians beat gongs and drums, and the people danced. When Adoko arrived in his hammock, carried by his slaves, he was taken three times around the city, then they brought him to his house. The royal stool was set in front of the house, and he sat there to watch the festivities.

Many bards were in the city for the celebration. They came before the new Chief and sang songs. The last of the bards to appear was the oldest of them all. In his lifetime he had seen many chiefs come and go, and it was he who knew how to recite the history of Adoko's family from the very beginning. They brought him before Adoko and asked him to sing. He tuned his lute and sang this song:

25

"Our new father is Adoko,
 He is great indeed,
 But our former Chief had no greatness.

Our new father is Adoko,
He is wise,
But our last Chief understood nothing.

Our new father is Adoko,
He is generous,
Even though our last Chief was stingy.

Adoko is our father,
He cares for the welfare of all,
But our last Chief did not care.

Nana Adoko is here,
He will judge our lawsuits with justice,
Our former Chief cared little for such things.

Our former Chief is gone,
He only slept and grew fat
Until he was claimed by death.

But Nana Adoko sleeps little,
He is our good father
Who watches over our affairs."

When Adoko heard this song of praise, he thought: "Indeed, I am the great Adoko. Who has ever said it so well? And my cousin, the Chief who has gone, was he not truly the poorest of rulers? How sharp and understanding these people are! How wise is this old bard!"

To the bard who had seen so many chiefs come and go, he said: "This song, it is good. It is a fine song. I shall make you the first singer of Agona as long as I live."

He ordered his servants to distribute gifts among all the people at the celebration and had palm wine given out.

Then he asked the old bard, "Who is the maker of the song you sang? He must be a great singer indeed. Are you the maker of this song?"

"Oh, no," the old bard answered. "I am not the composer. This song was made in ancient times, and we sing it each time a new Chief is appointed over us. We merely change the name of the Chief."

And when Adoko grew old and died, a bard sang to the new Chief:

"Our new father is Mahama,
  He is great indeed,
  But our former Chief had no greatness."

The Search: Who Gets the Chief's Daughter?

Ashanti Tribe, Ghana

HERE were three brothers who wanted to marry the same girl. She was the daughter of a powerful Chief. Each of the brothers made it known that he wished to have her.

The Chief called them to his house and said: "In the forest live the Mmoatia, the Little People. My daughter wants one of them to be her servant. Whichever of you first brings her one of the Little People, this man shall be her husband."

The three brothers went away and talked about what the Chief had said. One of them asked, "Wherever will we find the Mmoatia? Many people speak of them, but few people see them."

Another brother said, "Yes, who knows where they are to be found?"

And the third said, "Where their village is is not known to us, but it is somewhere in the great forest. Let us look for them."

Each of the brothers had special magic. The first had a magical mirror. If he looked into his mirror, he could see

things that were happening anywhere in the world. The second brother had a magic hammock, which would take him anywhere he wanted to go. The third brother had the power to bring the dead back to life.

They set out together to find the place where the Mmoatia lived. They traveled many days in the great forest. Whenever they met someone on the trail, they asked, "Do you know where the Mmoatia are to be found?" But no one could help them.

One day the first brother looked into his magic mirror, and he saw that the Chief's daughter had died. He told what he had seen. They said to each other, "Why should we search any longer for the Mmoatia? Now it is useless." They discussed it.

The third brother said, "I have the power to bring the dead back to life. If we could only return quickly, I could save her."

The second brother said, "I have the power to take us home. Enter my hammock."

The three brothers got into the hammock. It carried them back to their village instantly. They went to the Chief's house, and the third brother used his magic power and brought the Chief's daughter back to life.

Then the Chief declared:

"You searched in the forest; you did not find the Mmoatia. Yet you returned, and my daughter who had died, you brought her back to life. You are three, and all of you had a hand in it. But I have only one daughter. Only one of you can be my son-in-law. To the one who did the most, to him will I give my daughter."

One brother had seen in his mirror that the girl had died.

One had transported them back from the forest in his hammock.

One had revived the girl from death.

Which one deserved the reward?

The King's Drum

Ashanti Tribe, Ghana

HE King of the forest once called a meeting of all his subjects. His messengers went out to distant villages, and when the animals heard the King's command, they put on their best clothes and began their trip. But many weeks passed before they arrived.

When they had all gathered before his house, the King said to them: "When a meeting is called, many days pass before we are gathered. This is not good. What if we are in danger? What if the enemy is coming? We must find a way to gather quickly."

Anansi the spider was the King's counselor. He said, "What is needed is a drum. When the royal drum is beaten, it will be heard everywhere. Everyone will come quickly."

The animals applauded Anansi's suggestion. It was agreed that there should be a drum. The King ordered that a drum should be made. The animals were organized into work squads. Each squad was to take its turn at the making of the drum. First, one squad went out and cut a tree. Another squad went out to trim the tree. Another squad took adzes and cut the tree into the shape of a

drum. The drum was hollowed. After that, carvers were set
to work to decorate the drum. Only the monkey did not do
any work. While the others labored, the monkey found a
shady place and slept, or he went off looking for berries.
When they came back to the village, the animals sang:

> "Life is labor,
> We are tired,
> We are hot,
> It is for the King we labor."

The monkey also sang:

> "Life is labor,
> I am tired,
> I am hot,
> It is for the King I labor."

But Anansi saw that the monkey shirked and rested
while the others labored. He said nothing.

A time came when the drum was finished. The King announced: "Let the drum be brought in. There will be a
ceremony. The drum will be initiated. After that, the
assembly will be ended. When the people are wanted
again, the royal drum will be sounded."

Anansi said, "Yes, the drum shall be brought in. There
is only one problem remaining. Who shall carry the
drum?"

The drum was very large. It was heavy. The distance
was great. No one wanted to carry it.

The leopard said, "Let the lion receive the honor."

The lion said, "No, it is the antelope who should carry
it."

The antelope declared, "No, it is more fitting for the
elephant to do it."

Each animal suggested that another should have the honor.

Anansi said, "It appears that each person wants someone else to do the carrying. Therefore, I suggest that the person to carry the drum is he who is most lazy."

The King said, "Yes, that is the way to do it."

The animals considered the question. They looked at each other. They tried to think who was the laziest. First, one looked at the monkey, then another looked at the monkey. The monkey looked here, looked there. Everywhere he looked, he saw people looking at him.

He went to the middle of the crowd and said: "I wish to make a statement. I refuse to carry the drum. Never, never will I carry the drum. That is all I have to say."

All the animals laughed. The antelope said, "Why are you here? No one mentioned your name."

The porcupine said, "Why do you speak? No one asked you to carry the drum."

The crowd called out, "Yes, no one said even a word to him."

Once more the monkey said: "I want it to be made clear. I will not carry the drum. These are my words."

Again the animals laughed.

Anansi said to the King:

"No one mentioned the monkey's name. People were thinking to themselves, 'Who is the laziest?' They could not make up their minds. But the monkey was sure. He came forward. He said, 'I want it made clear that I will never carry the drum.' Thus he confessed that he is the laziest. With his own mouth he has said it."

The animals answered, "It is true, the monkey is the laziest of all!"

And so when at last the great drum was brought from the forest to the King's house, it was the monkey who carried it.

The Sky God's Daughter

Ashanti Tribe, Ghana

IT is said that Nyame, the Sky God, had a daughter whom many men wished to marry. Men came to Nyame, saying, "Your daughter, I wish to have her. Let us discuss a marriage settlement."

But Nyame turned them away, saying, "No, I cannot discuss it."

People said to each other, "Why does Nyame withhold his daughter? He will not even consider the matter." They talked about it in the market place. The old men pressed Nyame. They said, "It is not natural to do this. The matter should be discussed."

One day there was a big festival in the town. People danced, and Nyame danced. He had his stool brought out and he sat on it. He announced to the crowd:

"Many young men have asked for my daughter. To whom shall I give her? This is the heart of the matter. I have decided upon it. The first man who discovers my daughter's secret name, he shall be my son-in-law."

No one knew the name of Nyame's daughter. Men came to the Sky God and said, "Your daughter's name is So-and-so," but Nyame said, "No, that is not it," and sent them away.

Anansi the spider was at the festival. He decided he would marry the Sky God's daughter. He went to the garden where Nyame's daughter walked in the evening and he climbed a mango tree. There he waited. When the girl came walking with her servant, Anansi dropped a mango at their feet. The servant picked it up, saying, "Oh, Baduasemanpensa, a mango has fallen!" The girls ate the mango. Anansi dropped another one. The servant picked it up, saying, "Oh, Baduasemanpensa, another mango has fallen!" When the girls had eaten that one, Anansi dropped another. Each time the servant said, "Oh, Baduasemanpensa," Anansi repeated the name to himself.

When the girls left the garden, Anansi came down from the tree. All the way home he sang the name to himself so that he would not forget it. He did not close his eyes all night, fearing that he would lose the name if he slept. In the morning he went to the shrine of his ancestors and poured a libation of palm wine. He asked his ancestors to help him remember the name.

After that he took his talking drum from the wall and practiced playing "Baduasemanpensa" on it. He played it over and over: "Baduasemanpensa, Baduasemanpensa, Baduasemanpensa."

But his secret tormented him. He wished to tell someone. At last he went to another village where his friend Abosom the lizard lived. He told Abosom, "Nyame's daughter, her secret name is Baduasemanpensa. Nyame will give her to me. Come with me tomorrow. When Nyame says, 'What is her name?' I will play it on the talking drum, 'Baduasemanpensa, Baduasemanpensa.' Then Nyame will say, 'Anansi, he has told the name; he is my new son-in-law.'"

The next day Anansi sent a messenger to Nyame to tell him he was coming with the girl's name. Then he hung his drum on his shoulder, and with Abosom the lizard he went to Nyame's house.

Nyame, the Sky God, came out. His servants placed a stool for him, and he sat down.

"Your messenger came," Nyame said. "He said you will announce the name of my daughter. We are ready to hear it."

The whole town was there. People talked back and forth, saying, "Anansi is clever; he will announce the secret name," or, "Many men have tried and failed; is Anansi any different?"

Anansi took the drum from his shoulder and placed it under his arm. He began to play the name on it, over and over. After he had listened a while, Nyame said, "What is it the man is playing? I do not understand what the drum is saying."

People in the crowd said, "What is the drum talking about? We do not understand it."

Anansi played the drum harder and harder.

"What does the drum say?" the Sky God asked again.

"Surely you recognize it," Anansi replied, "It is the secret name of your daughter." And he continued to play.

At last the Sky God ordered him to stop. "Why do you waste my time? Tell me at once what the drum is supposed to be saying!"

Anansi turned to Abosom the lizard. He said, "Tell the people what the drum says. They are very stupid."

Abosom said, "The girl's name is Baduasemanpensa!"

The Sky God clapped his hands. "It is so! That is her name!"

The crowd made a great noise. They applauded.

Nyame, the Sky God, said: "It was promised that the man who revealed my daughter's name would be my son-in-law. My words are true. I therefore give my daughter to Abosom the lizard."

Anansi could hardly speak. He protested. "It was I who guessed your daughter's name! The lizard was only my translator!"

The Sky God replied: "I do not know what you were playing on the drum. Who could possibly understand such bad drumming? But we all heard Abosom the lizard say, 'Your daughter's name, it is Baduasemanpensa.' Therefore, Abosom is my son-in-law."

The crowd shouted, "Yes, it is truly spoken."

Thus it is said:

> "If you have important words to say,
>   Do not entrust them to the drum."

The Wedding of the Hawk

Ewe Tribe, Togo

THE hawk, when the time came, went out to find a wife for himself. He traveled from place to place, and at last he chose a girl in a distant village. He spoke to the girl's father, and arrangements were made. He gave presents to the girl's family. A time was set for the wedding, and the hawk then returned to his own house.

He gathered together all the gold dust he had saved and took it to a goldsmith to have a ring made. Because he was so good looking, some creatures envied the hawk and said things behind his back. They did not wish him well.

When the day of the wedding approached, the hawk went to the goldsmith for his ring, which he intended to give to his bride. Then he called for his friends to accompany him. His friend the lizard came. His friend the guinea fowl came. His friend the mantis came. His friend the snake came. Many others from his village joined the party.

They went to the house of the girl the hawk had chosen. All the necessary things were done. The hawk introduced his friends to the girl's family. There was drumming. There was singing. Then the hawk put his hand in his pocket for the ring to give it to his wife. The ring was not there. He searched through his clothes. He could not find it.

At last he cried out, "The ring has been stolen; it is gone!"

There was great excitement. The headman of the village said, "Let everyone be searched."

So everyone in the village was searched, but the ring was not found.

The hawk stood up. He spoke to the girl's father, saying, "I took all the gold dust that I had been saving, and I had a beautiful ring made. I brought it with me to give it to my wife, but someone who does not wish me well has stolen it from my pocket."

The father of the girl said, "Everyone has been searched. Yet the ring has not been found. You say so-and-so to explain it. Still, there is no ring, and a ring is needed. Therefore, the wedding cannot take place. When you have found the ring, we will talk of the matter again."

The hawk was overcome with shame. His friends, too, were ashamed. The lizard was speechless; he could not find his voice. He only moved his head from side to side as though to say, "Oh, what a terrible thing!"

The guinea fowl clapped his hands violently against his head, saying, "Disgrace, disgrace!"

The mantis kept hitting his sides with his fists, saying, "Oh, no, it cannot be true!"

And the snake opened his mouth and put out his tongue, turning this way and that to show everyone that he did not have the ring there.

The hawk and his friends went away. "I will search for

the person who stole the ring," the hawk said. He flew into the air and soared over the countryside, looking for the thief.

As for the lizard, he has never spoken a word since that day. He simply moves his head from side to side as though to say, "Oh, what a terrible thing!" Because the guinea fowl clapped his hands so hard against his head, his head became bald, and so it remained. Because the mantis struck his sides so hard with his fists, he became very thin, like a walking stick. And the snake, whenever he meets someone, opens his mouth and puts his tongue out to show that he doesn't have the ring hidden there.

The hawk has never given up his search. He forever soars and hovers in the sky, diving down now and then upon some moving creature to see if it is wearing the missing ring.

How Poverty Was Revealed to
the King of Adja

Dahomey

ADJAHOSU, the King of Adja, had everything.

One day he went to see his diviner. He said to him, "You must divine something for me. I am too rich and do not know what it is to be poor. I want to know what it is to be poor."

The diviner took his divining shells; he threw them on the earth and studied them. Many times he tossed the shells and read their meaning. Then he told the King of Adja to bring him a drum, a gong, and rattles. He told the King of Adja to have his hunters catch a giraffe.

When the King returned home, he gathered the drum, the gong, and the rattles and sent his hunters to catch the giraffe, as the diviner had instructed him. When everything that was needed was ready, Adjahosu brought them to the diviner.

The diviner told them to tie the gong, drum, and rattles around the neck of the giraffe and instructed Adjahosu to get on its back. Then they took a cloth and tied him in place, and the diviner gave him a little stick with which to strike the drum. When Adjahosu beat the drum, the giraffe ran away with him into the bush.

45

They passed through brush and thorny bushes until they were in the middle of the forest, where the cloth that tied the King became so torn that it broke, and the King fell to the ground. He did not know where his house was. He was completely lost.

As he could find no place to sleep, he climbed a tree and stayed there throughout the night. He was in the forest three months. He ate only what he could find. One day he had an accident and lost an eye.

At the end of the third month, he came upon an old woman looking for leaves of the indigo plant in the forest. When the old woman looked at him, it seemed to her that he was completely blind. She led him to her house. He became her servant. And every five days, when the woman went to market to sell the cloth she had dyed, she put the load on Adjahosu's head and led him there. When she sold her dyed cloth and bought new cloth to dye, she placed the load on Adjahosu's head and led him home.

This she did for three years.

In the meantime, the children of the King of Adja did not know what had happened to him. One day, however, the woman went to one of the King's fields to sell something to some of his sons. As usual, Adjahosu carried the cloths. When they reached the King's field, his sons looked at the man who was with the old woman. He had only one eye, but he resembled their father.

While they watched, someone called out to the man, "Adjahosu, come and sell me some wood."

When the sons returned home, they went to their eldest brother and said, "Look, we were at the market in the field of Adjahosu, and we saw a man whom they call Adjahosu. And an old woman commanded him to sell wood."

The older brother said, "Good, we will go to the next market there."

So he went early to the next market and arrived before the old woman came. He placed himself where his younger brothers had been, and after a time he saw her coming, accompanied by a man who was carrying her cloths. When the man put the cloths down, he took his bush knife and entered the nearby forest. In a short time he returned with wood, which he put down beside the old woman. After this she said, "You can eat," and gave him something to eat.

As he was eating, his son approached him. When he recognized his child, Adjahosu began to cry, and the son cried also.

The son led his father to the old woman and asked her, "Where did you find this man?"

She answered, "I was looking for indigo leaves. One day I saw him alone in the forest."

The son took the man and said, "Now you will sell him to me."

She said, "If I sell him now, who will carry my load to my house?"

The son said, "I will buy him and give you the money, and you can buy another carrier with this money."

The woman said, "Let me be! This old one here, what will you do with him?"

The son replied, "This is not an old one to me. He is my father. I beg you to sell him to me."

The old woman said, "Since he is your father, take him."

So his son took Adjahosu home and bathed him and gave him fresh clothes.

After that Adjahosu summoned all his people before him to speak to them. He said: "Because I myself am very, very rich, I wanted to know what poverty is. Now I say to you, my sons and my family, never ask to be poor, because poverty eats nothing, drinks nothing."

And so it is said: "A man must not seek poverty."

Three Sons of a Chief

Hausa Tribe, Nigeria

HERE was a Chief, and he had three sons. Each of them was greatly talented in the art of fighting. Each was talented in the art of riding.

One day the Chief called his people together before his house. He announced that he was going to test his sons to see which one of them had the greatest skill.

To his sons he said, "Here, at this baobab tree that stands by our house, let us see which of you is the most talented."

The sons mounted their horses. They rode away for a distance and stopped.

The eldest son tried his skill first. He galloped his horse toward the baobab tree, thrust his spear through the great tree, and rode his horse through the hole that it made. He rode on.

The second son came next. He galloped his horse forward, and when he came to the tree, he caused his horse to leap over it. He rode on.

The youngest son was next. He rode forward, seized the baobab tree in his hand, and pulled it from the earth, roots and all. He rode on, waving the great tree aloft.

Now, who was the greatest among the three? If you do not know, that is all.

The Brave Man of Gola

Hausa Tribe, Nigeria

A man named Seidu lived in the village of Golo. Whenever the men of his village went hunting and returned with game, Seidu said to his wife: "Among all the hunters, I was the bravest. Singlehanded I fought with the leopard and chased the elephant. I went forward with my spear, and the lion fled. I am the bravest of hunters."

His wife, Ladi, replied, "Did no one but you bring back meat?"

Seidu said, "Yes, because of my fearlessness, the others also had good luck."

Again, when it was said that the enemy was approaching, Seidu went into the bush country with the men, and when he returned, he hung his spear on the wall and said to his wife: "The enemy came forward; I went forward. When I ran at them, they turned and fled. My reputation has spread everywhere. I am the bravest of warriors. What is your opinion?"

Ladi answered, "It is so."

There was a funeral one time in another village, and some of the women of Golo wished to go. But the men were working in the fields and could not leave their work.

51

Ladi told the women, "My husband is the bravest of men. He will take us through the forest."

She went to Seidu, saying, "The women who are going to the funeral agree that you are the one to take them through the forest. Will you go?"

Seidu said, "From one day to another no one mentions my courage. But when courage is needed, people ask, 'Where is Seidu?' Nevertheless, I will come."

He took his spear and went with the women through the forest.

There were warriors of the enemy in the forest. They were hunting game. When they saw Seidu coming with the women, they said, "Look how the man struts like a guinea cock. Let us strike fear into him."

They waited near the trail, and when the people of Golo came, the hunters came out of the brush before them and behind them.

Seidu shouted, "We are surrounded! Run for the trees!"

The women ran among the trees. Seidu ran with them. But there were enemy among the trees, and they seized all the people from Golo.

The leader of the hunters said to Seidu's wife, "What is your name?"

She replied, "Ladi."

He said, "Ladi is a name used by the women of our tribe also. Because you are called Ladi, we shall not hurt you."

He said to another woman, "What is your name?"

Seeing how good it was to be named Ladi, the woman replied: "My name too is Ladi."

The leader of the hunters said, "A good name; we shall not hurt you."

He asked another woman, and she too replied, "Ladi." All of the women were asked, and all of them answered, "My name is Ladi."

Then the leader of the hunters spoke to Seidu. "All the women of your village are named Ladi. It is a strange custom. In our village each woman has a different name. But you, guinea cock who leads the guinea hens, what are you called?"

"I," Seidu said, "I too am called Ladi. My name is Ladi also."

When the hunters heard Seidu's reply, they laughed. The leader of the hunters declared, "No, it is not possible. Ladi is a woman's name. You are a man with a spear. Do not tell me that the men of your village are also called Ladi?"

Seidu said, "No, no, only the women are called Ladi."

The hunters said, "How then are you called Ladi?"

Seidu looked one way and another way, but he saw no chance of escape. He said, "You see, appearances are deceiving. I also am a woman."

The enemy laughed. They could not stop laughing. The women of Golo laughed too.

Seidu's wife spoke. She said, "He speaks badly of himself. He is the courageous Seidu, the famous Seidu."

Seidu said then, "Yes, it is so."

A hunter said, "People say that Seidu claims to be the bravest of all men."

"No," Seidu replied, "it is no longer so. *Formerly* I was the bravest of all men. Today it is different. From now on I shall be only the bravest in my village."

The hunters let them go. Seidu and the women went to the funeral, and they returned afterwards to their own

houses. When they arrived in Golo, everyone was laughing at Seidu. Instead of calling him by his name, they
called him Ladi. He went into his house and closed the
door. Whenever he came out, they laughed. He could not
hide from the shame.

At last he sent his wife to tell them this: "Seidu who
was formerly the bravest of men was reduced to being
the bravest in his village. But from now on he is not the
bravest in the village. He agrees to be only as brave as
other people."

So the people of Golo stopped ridiculing Seidu. And
thereafter he was no braver than anyone else.

The Feast

Bamum Tribe, Cameroun

A Chief who ruled over many villages decided to give a great feast for all of his people. So he sent messengers to the villages to announce the event. His messengers told the people that the feast would take place on such and such a day and asked each of the men to bring one calabash of palm wine.

The day of the festival came. People bathed and dressed in their best clothes. They walked to the Chief's village. Many hundreds of men and their families were on the roads and paths. They converged on the house of the Chief. There was drumming and dancing. Each man, as he entered the Chief's compound, went with his calabash to a large earthen pot, into which he poured the liquid refreshment that he had brought.

Now there was one man who wanted very much to attend the feast, but he had no palm wine to bring. His wife said, "Why don't you buy palm wine from so-and-so, who has plenty?"

But the man replied, "What! Spend money so that I can attend a feast that is free? No, there must be another way."

And after a while he said to his wife, "Hundreds and hundreds of people will pour their wine into the Chief's pot. Could one calabash of water spoil so much wine? Who would know the difference?"

And so he filled his calabash with water and went with the others to the Chief's village. When he arrived, he saw the guests pouring their wine into the big pot, and he went forward and poured his water there and greeted the Chief. Then he went to where the men were sitting, and he sat with them to await the serving of the palm wine.

When all the guests had arrived, the Chief ordered his servants to fill everyone's cups. The cups were filled, and each of the men awaited the signal to begin to drink. The man who had brought only water was impatient, for there was nothing so refreshing as palm wine.

The Chief gave the signal, and the guests put the cups to their lips. They tasted. They tasted again. And what they tasted was not palm wine but water, for each of them had thought, "One calabash of water cannot spoil a great pot of good palm wine." And each of them had filled his calabash at the spring. Thus the large earthen pot contained nothing but water, and it was water they had to drink at the Chief's feast.

So it is said among the people: "When only water is brought to the feast, it is water that must be drunk."

Frog's Wives Make Ndiba Pudding

Bakongo Tribe, Republic of the Congo

T is said that the frog had first one wife and that then he took another, making two. The first wife, he built a house for her in Ndumbi, and he cleared fields there and had a garden. The second wife, he built her a house in Ndala, and there too he cleared fields for a garden. Frog then left the gardens to his wives and went to visit with the men. When he was in Ndumbi, caring for his yams, he ate with his first wife. When he was in Ndala caring for his trees, he ate with his second wife.

Once when the frog was elsewhere talking with the men, a messenger came from his first wife. He said: "Oh, Frog, your wife in Ndumbi has just prepared *ndiba* pudding, and she wants you to come at once and eat."

As the messenger from Ndumbi finished speaking, another messenger came from his second wife, saying: "Oh, Frog, your wife in Ndala has just made *ndiba* pudding, and she waits for you to come and eat."

The frog had great fondness for *ndiba* pudding. He was very happy, for both wives had prepared it for him. Yet each wife wanted him to come at once. Ndumbi was an hour to the north. Ndala was an hour to the south. To eat

first at Ndumbi was to make his second wife wait till nightfall for him to come. To eat first at Ndala was to make his first wife wait till nightfall.

"If I go first to Ndumbi," the frog said, "my second wife will be sharp with me. She will say I am catering to the eldest because she is nicer. If I go first to Ndala, my first wife will greet me later with endless stinging words; she will say I favor the youngest because of her beauty. Oh, I am in trouble! Which way shall I go?"

But he went neither one way nor the other. He stayed where he was, fearing to go either to Ndumbi or Ndala.

So it is that the frog croaks, "Gaou! Gaou!" at all hours of the day or night. He is saying, "I am in trouble, I am in trouble!"

All this came about because frog's two wives made *ndiba* pudding and both sent for him at the same time.

Two Friends: How They Parted

Bakongo Tribe, Republic of the Congo

N ancient times the chameleon and the monkey were friends; they had drunk together from the same bowl. Where one went, the other went. What one had, the other shared. Now it is different. Each goes his separate way, and when they meet they do not greet each other. If the chameleon sees the monkey coming, he goes in the tall grass or hides behind a tree. If the monkey encounters the chameleon, he ignores him.

Once in the old days, when they were friends, the monkey said to the chameleon, "Let us go away from this place to another country. Here food is difficult to find. In that other place beyond the river, we will surely find all that we need to eat."

The chameleon said, "Yes, let us go."

They began their journey. They went beyond the river and crossed the grasslands. The distance was great. They walked, walked, walked.

They heard a man calling to them. He said, "You people, what are you doing here?"

The monkey and the chameleon replied, "We are walking. We came from one place and we are going to another."

The man came to them and said, "I am the palm-wine maker here. Last night I hung twenty calabashes on my palm trees to catch juice for my wine. But this morning the calabashes are empty. Which one of you stole the juice?"

The chameleon replied, "No, we are not to blame."

The palm-wine maker said, "One of you has stolen the juice from the calabashes. Must I beat you both for it?"

The monkey became fearful. He said to the palm-wine maker, "That man there, the chameleon, must have drunk the juice. See, it has made him sleepy; his eyes are only half open. And how slowly he walks. He is afraid he will fall down. His head, see how it moves from side to side. It is clear that he is stupified by the palm-wine juice."

"Yes," the palm-wine maker said, "who can deny it?"

He struck the chameleon with a stick. He beat the chameleon until he was almost dead. When the palm-wine maker went away, the chameleon could hardly move his bruised body. But the monkey only laughed.

The chameleon said, "You are my friend. We drank together from the same bowl. He beat me until I almost died. You did not help me. You only laughed."

"Friend chameleon," the monkey replied, "I am small. Am I a match for a man? Yes, I laughed, but all the time I was suffering with you. I laughed only to hide my grief."

The chameleon said no more. They walked again. And when they had gone a great distance, they saw smoke and fire. A man called to them, saying, "You people, what are you doing here?"

They replied, "Only walking. We have come from one place and are going to another."

The man came to where they stood and asked, "Which of you set fire to my trees and gardens?"

The monkey spoke out quickly, saying, "We are not to blame. We have just arrived in this country."

The farmer said, "My corn has been scorched. My family's trees have been burned. You evil people, admit your crime!"

The monkey could not speak. He was terrified. But the chameleon said, "Indeed, this is a crime. How can an honest man remain silent? Look at the palms of our hands. If one has played with fire, his hands will be black with soot. If either of us has done this evil thing, the mark of the soot will surely be seen."

"It is true," the farmer said.

He looked first at the palms of the chameleon's hands. They were clean. Then he looked at the palms of the monkey's hands. They were black.

"Here is the criminal!" the farmer said, and he seized hold of the monkey.

"No, no!" the monkey protested. "This has always been the color of my hands! This is the way it is with all of my tribe!"

"Speak no more silly words," the farmer said. "Your hands are the color of soot. It is you who have set my fields afire."

He struck the monkey, and beat him again and again with a stick. When the man went away, the monkey lay motionless and silent. Then little by little he began to move and the power of speech returned. The chameleon laughed.

"You are my friend," the monkey said, "but the man tried to kill me, and you laughed. Go your way. I shall go mine."

Thus the chameleon and the monkey parted. One went one way; the other went another. In the beginning they were friends; they drank from the same bowl. But thenceforth, they had nothing to do with one another.

It is always this way: A person who laughs at another person's misfortune can expect to be laughed at when he is in trouble.

The Hunter and His Talking Leopard

Bakongo Tribe, Republic of the Congo

A leopard prowling near a village fell into a trap set by a hunter. There the leopard was caught; he could not escape. When the hunter came and saw that he had caught a leopard, he was delighted. He danced around the trap, saying, "Ah, Leopard, you have fallen into my trap! There it was, plain to see, yet you walked into it! It is stupidity that has brought you to this fate!"

The leopard answered him, saying, "It is stupidity that brought me here. Cleverness will bring you here too."

The hunter said in surprise, "Why, the leopard talks! Whoever before has caught a talking leopard? Who ever heard of such a thing?"

He hurried to the village, calling out to the people, "I have caught a leopard that talks, I have caught a leopard that talks!" The people gathered around him, and he said, "I set my trap at the edge of the forest. A leopard came and fell into it. I spoke to him, saying, 'Oh, but you are stupid,' and he replied to me."

People said to each other, "He lies. There is no such thing as a leopard that talks."

"It is true that other leopards do not talk," the hunter

said. "But this one speaks. As we are here talking together, just so the leopard and I had a conversation."

People said, "This man lies. Leopards do not speak the language of men."

The hunter said, "If I lie, I will move my house from the village. If he does not speak, I will live forever out

there on the edge of the forest where I have set my traps."

The people said, "Your words, we shall remember them. As you have said it, so it shall be. Let us go."

They went together in a crowd to where the leopard was caught in the trap. The hunter approached the leopard and said to him, "You who are caught in the trap, it is stupidity that brought you here." But the leopard did not reply. The man said again, "You, spotted one, your stupidity brought you here." The leopard remained silent. The man poked at the leopard with his staff, saying once more, "You, Leopard, speak! It is stupidity that brought you here!" But the leopard said nothing.

After a while the people said: "Man, you lied. You said, 'The leopard speaks.' You said, 'If he does not speak, may I live forever in the forest instead of the village.' These words you gave us from your own mouth. Therefore, do not return to the village. Build your house here."

And the villagers went back to the village, leaving the hunter behind.

The hunter said to the leopard, "Oh, you foolish one, why didn't you speak? You spoke before, and when I brought witnesses, you were speechless."

The leopard spoke then. He said, "It is my stupidity that brought me here. You, it is your cleverness that brought you here. One of us was too foolish. The other was too clever. We end up in the same place."

So it is said: "Too foolish and too clever, they are brothers."

The Past and the Future

Mbaka Tribe, Angola

Two men were walking together on the road. They met a tapper of palm wine, and they said to him, "Please give us palm wine to drink, we are thirsty."

The tapper said to them, "Before I give you palm wine, first tell me your names."

The first man answered, "I am Whence-We-Come."

The second man answered, "I am Where-We-Go."

The palm wine tapper said, "Whence-We-Come, you have a beautiful name. Here, I will give you palm wine. But you, Where-We-Go, have an evil name. You are no good. Therefore, I will not give you palm wine."

They began to quarrel. The argument became heated. So they went to find a man to judge their dispute. Each of them told his story. The judge listened. Then he said:

"The tapper is wrong. Where-We-Go is right, because what is behind us, we cannot get anything more from there. The thing we shall find is where we are going."

The tapper said, "It is so." And he gave palm wine to Where-We-Go.

The Elephant Hunters
Mbaka Tribe, Angola

KINGUNGU, the hunter, said, "I will go in the forest to hunt game." He took up his gun, went into the forest, and stalked the elephants. After much walking, he came close to the elephant herd. He shot one elephant, it fell on the ground.

Another hunter, Ndala, from the same village, was in the forest. He saw Kingungu stalking the elephants. He followed him. He heard Kingungu fire his weapon, and he ran to where Kingungu's elephant lay on the ground. Ndala fired his gun at the elephant and cried out, "This elephant is mine."

Kingungu came to Ndala and said: "This elephant is mine. I stalked it. I shot it with my gun. You came and found it lying on the ground. Why do you cry out now, saying the elephant is yours?"

The two hunters quarreled in the forest. Kingungu said, "The elephant is mine."

Ndala said, "The elephant is mine."

At last they said, "Let us go to the village; there we shall be judged to see who is right."

They returned to the village, and Kingungu went to

the headman. He accused Ndala. The headman sent for Ndala, and when he came, the two hunters pleaded their cases.

Kingungu said: "I stalked the elephant herd. I went here, I went there. Wherever the elephant herd went, I followed. I approached, I shot my elephant. Then came Ndala. He saw my elephant lying on the ground. He shot it, saying, 'This is my elephant.'"

Ndala said, "I followed the elephant, I shot it. It is mine. Why then does Kingungu claim it?"

The headman said: "How can I judge who is right and who is wrong? There were no witnesses there in the forest to say one man speaks the truth and the other speaks an untruth. Let us wait. Tomorrow I will decide the case."

They separated then. The sun went down, it was night.

Kingungu went into the forest where his elephant was. Ndala followed him. Kingungu began to cry out in a loud voice, "This elephant is my elephant! This elephant is my elephant!"

Ndala began to cry out too, "This elephant is my elephant! This elephant is my elephant!"

Ndala cried out this way for one hour. Then he was tired of crying out, and he went away.

But Kingungu kept on crying, "This elephant is my elephant! This elephant is my elephant!" He stayed there all night with the elephant.

The morning came, and the headman sent for Kingungu and Ndala. When they arrived, he said, "Plead your cases again." Kingungu told his story again. Ndala told his story again. The headman said to the people, "Who was it who stayed with the elephant all night, crying, 'This elephant is my elephant'?"

The people said, "Kingungu stayed all night with the elephant. Ndala, he stayed an hour, then he became tired and left."

The headman said: "It is clear. Kingungu is right. Ndala is wrong. Kingungu hunted, he shot his elephant. Ndala wanted an elephant the easy way, he would not work for it. Kingungu stayed all night crying, 'This is my elephant.' Ndala stayed only an hour. He still wanted the elephant the easy way. Ndala wanted wrongly to take Kingungu's elephant. The elephant belongs to Kingungu."

A Father-in-Law and His Son-in-Law

Loanda Dialect, Angola

NE night a father-in-law and his son-in-law were sitting outside the house enjoying the evening air. It grew dark, and the father-in-law got up from where he sat, saying, "My son-in-law, let us go to sleep. The darkness is like the gloom of a blind eye."

His son-in-law was overcome with shame, for he was blind in one eye, but he said nothing.

Another night when the moon was in the sky, the father-in-law and the son-in-law were again outside the house talking. The son-in-law then said, "Oh, sir, let us go to sleep, for the moon is shining like a bald head; it will do us harm sitting here."

The father-in-law, who was bald, was afflicted with shame. He went silently into his house. He did not say good night to his son-in-law. The son-in-law also went into his house.

In three days the father-in-law went to six aged men of the village. He said, "I want to complain about the insult which my son-in-law gave me." The aged men sent for the son-in-law. When the son-in-law arrived, the father-in-law spoke. He said:

"My son-in-law and I were sitting outside in the night. He saw the moon rise. He would not say merely, 'Let us go to sleep.' Instead, he spoke with a heart to offend me, saying, 'There is a moonlight like the shine of a bald head. Let us go to sleep, father-in-law, for this moonlight will do us harm.' Therefore, I am not his friend because of the insults he gave me. I am bald-headed. He said, 'Bald-head shine.' Did he not insult me? Therefore I reject friendship with him."

Then the son-in-law spoke. He said:

"I would not have said it if my father-in-law had not first insulted me. One day after dark we were outside talking. My father-in-law told me, 'Come, let us go to sleep, for there is a darkness like the gloom of a blind eye.' I am blind in one eye. You, gentlemen, did he not insult me?"

They said to the son-in-law:

"It is the truth. He insulted you."

To the father-in-law they said:

"Why did you say this thing about the darkness to your son-in-law? If he said the moon is like a bald-head shine, he only returned the insult you gave him in the beginning. Your son-in-law was blind in his eye when you accepted him for your daughter. It is said, 'When a thing is bought, do not refer to it.' You knew your son-in-law was blind in one eye. You referred to it. Now when he pays you back, shall it be a crime?"

The aged men said:

"Father-in-law and son-in-law, do not be enemies. You, father-in-law, have no son. Your son-in-law is your son. You yourself were the first to offend; then he answered you. Be friends. Do not go away with this affair the way it is, take it out of your heart. We will not hate each other because of these things. Bring rum, let us drink. We will have no bad words."

The father-in-law and the son-in-law drank together. They remained in friendship.

The Donkeys Ask for Justice
Ethiopia

N former times the sky and the earth were close to one another. The hyena and his tribe lived in the sky. The donkey and his tribe lived on the earth and were not servants of man in those days.

The hyena had a fine, strong voice, and when he sang he was heard on the earth below. The donkeys were very pleased with the sound, and through their Chief they called out to God, saying: "In the sky there is one with a beautiful voice. The people of our tribe say to each other, 'Why should the one with the beautiful voice live in the sky? Let him come to the earth.'"

God considered the matter, and he agreed. He sent the hyena and his tribe to live on the earth.

The hyena then notified the donkeys that he had arrived and that he would receive them at his house. On the day that was set, the donkeys came. When they reached the gate, a servant of the hyena told them: "Our Chief, the one with the beautiful voice, has invited you to meet with him. As a token of your appreciation, you must leave a piece of your upper lip with me as you enter."

So every donkey, when it entered, gave a piece of its upper lip to the gatekeeper. They took their places in the house and asked the hyena to sing for them. He sang, and they were pleased. But when they smiled and tried to show their pleasure, their upper teeth were exposed in an unnatural way because of the piece of lip each had given to the gatekeeper.

The hyena said to them, "What is the matter? Why do you sneer at me when I sing?"

They answered, "We are only showing our pleasure." And they smiled again.

The hyena cried out: "They are still sneering. They speak soft words and insult me with their teeth! In our own house they provoke us! Oh, young men! Oh, warriors! Take up your weapons and punish them! Make them flee in terror! Kill them and scatter their bones everywhere!"

The donkeys fled from the hyena's house. Some were caught and killed by the hyena and his tribe. The others, who escaped, came to a place where a man was threshing grain in his fields. They cried out to him, "Save us from the hyenas!"

The man answered, "I have been working in my fields all day. I am tired. I cannot go to war against the hyenas."

The Chief of the donkeys said, "If you will protect us from the hyenas, we shall be your servants. We shall carry your heavy loads for you."

"Very well," the man answered, "it is agreed. So it will be."

He made rope from grass and bags from leather. He filled the bags with grain and tied them on the donkeys' backs, and they carried for him. When the hyenas came

searching for the donkeys, the man drove them away with his spear.

The news spread that donkeys were carrying grain for the farmer. Other men came to see it, because before this men had to carry their own grain. Everyone wanted donkeys, so the farmer gave them away, one here, one there, saving only one for himself. In this way, because they needed protection from the hyenas, donkeys became slaves to men.

But their work was very hard. Their loads were heavy. They carried from morning till night. Their backs ached. So they went to their Chief and asked him to appeal to God for help. The Chief of the donkeys departed to visit

God to complain of their slavery. But on the way he was caught and devoured by the hyenas.

Time passed. He did not return. The donkeys asked one another, "Has there been any word from our Chief? When will God give us justice? When will we be released from our slavery?"

This happened long ago. The donkeys are weary. They still are waiting for their Chief to return. They have not forgotten. Whenever two donkeys meet on the trail, they stop and put their noses together, and one of them asks, "What is the news? Has our Chief come back? Is there any message?"

And the other answers, "No, not yet. We are still waiting."

Even though their masters are impatient with them when they stop, and beat them with a stick or twist their tails to make them move, the donkeys stand together until they have finished their conversation. Then they move on until they meet other donkeys, and again the question is asked, "Is their any word from our Chief?" To this day they hope for release from their slavery.

And if they seem to sneer when they talk, it is only because they left a piece of their upper lip with the hyena's gatekeeper.

The Lion's Share
Somalia

HE lion, the jackal, the wolf, and the hyena had a meeting and agreed that they would hunt together in one party and share equally among them whatever game they caught.

They went out and killed a camel. The four animals then discussed which one of them would divide the meat. The lion said, "Whoever divides the meat must know how to count."

Immediately the wolf volunteered, saying, "Indeed, I know how to count."

He began to divide the meat. He cut off four pieces of equal size and placed one before each of the hunters.

The lion was angered. He said, "Is this the way to count?" And he struck the wolf across the eyes, so that his eyes swelled up and he could not see.

The jackal said, "The wolf does not know how to count. I will divide the meat."

He cut three portions that were small and a fourth portion that was very large. The three small portions he placed before the hyena, the wolf, and himself. The large portion he put in front of the lion, who took his meat and went away.

"Why was it necessary to give the lion such a large piece?" the hyena said. "Our agreement was to divide and share equally. Where did you ever learn how to divide?"

"I learned from the wolf," the jackal answered.

"Wolf? How can anyone learn from the wolf? He is stupid," the hyena said.

"The jackal was right," the wolf said. "He knows how to count. Before, when my eyes were open, I did not see it. Now, though my eyes are wounded, I see it clearly."

Nawasi Goes to War
Somalia

A merchant named Nawasi and his servant were traveling from Hargheisa to the south. They came to a watering hole, where they stopped to fill their water bags and let their horses drink. While they rested there, a party of warriors rode up. Nawasi greeted them, but they did not answer him. They said to each other, "Who is this person without weapons?" These men were Adama warriors who had been in battle, and in time of war all men wore their leather girdles and carried their spears and shields. When they had watered their horses, the Adama warriors rode away without a word to Nawasi.

Later in the day Nawasi and his servant passed another party of warriors. Nawasi greeted them, but again someone said, "Who but a woman carries no shield or spear?"

Nawasi said to his servant: "In this country a man who is not a hero is nobody. So I shall be a hero. Let us camp here. Go out and find me a shield and weapons."

While Nawasi rested, his servant went out to the Adama villages to buy weapons. When he returned, he brought a leather shield, several spears, and a leather girdle.

Nawasi put on the girdle, hung the shield on his saddle, held a spear in his hand, and they rode off.

Another war party came by, and Nawasi greeted them. The warriors looked at his shield, which was battered, and at his spear, which was sharp, and they answered his greeting.

Nawasi came to an Adama town. Night was falling. He called to his servant to announce his arrival. The servant took out his lyre and played on it, singing:

> "Who is more fierce than the hero Nawasi?
>   He has scattered the Haweia in battle!
>   He has brought them terror!
>   He has brought them death!"

When the townspeople heard the singing, they came and stood in respect before Nawasi to welcome him.

"Look," one of them said, "see the scars of battle on his leather girdle!"

"Yes," another said, "see the marks on his shield where he has received the blows of the enemy!"

"Ah," another said, "see the powerful right arm that wields the spear!"

Nawasi's servant sang again:

> "The blows of the Haweia fall like rain,
>   But Nawasi's blows fall like thunder!
>   The Haweia warriors fall like chaff on the ground,
>   And Nawasi insults their corpses!"

Nawasi thrust his spear into the ground. "I am tired, I have fought, I will rest," he said.

The people answered, "He is the hero Nawasi, he has defeated the Haweia, let him rest here." And they gave

Nawasi a house to rest in and brought cooked goat meat for them to eat.

Nawasi said to his servant, "A man who is not a hero is nobody. Let us sleep."

So they slept.

The sun was just rising when there was a great clamor at the door. The people shouted: "Awake, Hero Nawasi! The Haweia are coming to fight! Our men are gathering to meet them on the hill!"

Nawasi said in great alarm, "Where shall I go?"

And the people cried out, "To the hill! To the hill!"

Because they had never before seen a great hero prepare for battle, the Adama people stood and waited.

Nawasi's anguish was great. He could hardly speak. He called to his servant, saying, "Tell them the truth, tell them who I am!"

His servant took up his lyre and began to sing:

"Who is he who is awakened from his rest?
It is Nawasi, the slayer of the Haweia dogs!
Nawasi, who makes widows of Haweia women!
Nawasi, who makes orphans of their children!"

Nawasi groaned. The people shouted: "The Haweia are coming! Our men are going out! Great Nawasi, they need you!" And they brought his horse before the door.

Nawasi said: "Has the horse been saddled?"

They answered: "Yes, he is saddled."

Nawasi said: "Has he been bridled?"

They replied: "Yes, he is bridled."

Nawasi said faintly: "But has he been bridled correctly?"

They cried out together: "Yes, he is ready!"

Nawasi slowly put on his leather girdle. He looked at his servant, saying, "Tell them who I really am."

The servant took his lyre again and sang:

"Whose is the battle-scarred girdle of leather?
Whose is the iron arm that parries the blows?
Whose is the horse bridled for war?
They belong to the hero Nawasi, from Hargheisa!"

The people were waiting. Nawasi mounted the horse. He took the leather lines in his hand. But he did not go. At last he said, "Give me my shield." They gave him his shield. The horse began to walk.

"Look!" the people shouted. "The hero goes to war even without a spear!"

Nawasi stopped the horse. "Yes, the spear," he said. "Give me my spear."

His servant gave him a spear. Nawasi sat, watching the Adama warriors riding up the hill to meet the Haweia.

He said to his servant, "Has my horse been fed?"

"Yes, the horse has been fed."

"Has he been watered?"

"Yes, he has been watered."

"Very well," Nawasi said, "now I am going. Let them beware."

And his servant sang:

"Oh, you Haweia dogs on the hill,
Turn and scatter before it is too late!
For Nawasi comes on his white horse!
Nawasi, the conqueror from the north!"

"One moment," Nawasi said, "give me another spear." His servant gave him another spear.

"Are there no more?" Nawasi asked.

"Yes, here is the third," his servant said, and gave it to him.

Nawasi sat thus, girdled for war, his shield on one side and three spears under his arm. The battle was raging on the hill.

"My leather girdle, where is it?" Nawasi asked faintly.

"You are wearing it," his servant said. And then Nawasi's horse began to walk slowly out of the town. The servant sang:

> "The Haweia hyenas are doomed!
> Their weapons shall litter the hills!
> Their bones shall bleach in the sun!
> For the great Nawasi comes like a storm!"

Nawasi's horse came to the foot of the hill, and there it stopped and began to graze.

"Ah, you horse!" Nawasi said. "Are you a warrior's mount or a miserable beast of burden? While the heroes fight, you fill your belly!"

An Adama warrior rode down from the hill to see what was wrong.

"Oh, this creature that calls itself a horse!" Nawasi cried out. "He has no fighting spirit!"

"You are not holding the lines," the Adama man said. "You must steer him by the bit." And he rode back to the battle.

Nawasi dropped his spears on the ground and took the lines in his hands. He steered the horse this way and that, to the left, to the right. Suddenly he saw a party of horsemen galloping toward him from the battlefield. He wheeled and rode back into the town, calling out: "The battle is over! Flee for your lives! The Haweia are upon us!"

When he came to his house, he jumped from his horse and called to his servant:

"The Haweia are coming!"

He lay down on his sleeping mat and said to his servant: "Quickly! Pull a cover over me! When the enemy arrives, tell them I died last night in my sleep!"

The servant covered him with a cloth.

The warriors arrived. They were Adama men. There was much noise. Weapons rattled. People shouted. They came into Nawasi's house.

"The war is over," they said. "The Haweia have fled."

Nawasi sat up and threw off the cover.

"Ah!" he said. "The Haweia dogs saw me coming! How wisely they chose to return whence they came!"

Nawasi's servant took up his lyre and sang:

"How wise are the Haweia!
  The sight of Nawasi brought them to their senses!
  How fortunate they are!
  They have not felt his iron blows!"

Ruda, the Quick Thinker

Sudan

A trader by the name of Ruda went from Khartoum to the sea, and there he embarked on a sailing ship bound for Arabia. Among his own people Ruda had been known for his quickness of mind. Whenever there was a great problem, Ruda did not say, "Well, on the one hand, let us do this, and on the other hand, perhaps we should do that." He was decisive. He made decisions quickly, and once they had been made, he no longer tortured himself about things.

When the ship was at sea, Ruda stood at the rail, talking to another trader. The two men exchanged gossip and then began to discuss the valuable articles they had to sell. Ruda said, "Among my articles is a necklace and breastplate made by the most famous goldsmith of Khartoum. It is worth as much as the whole city of Aden."

"Is it so? I would like to see this treasure," the other trader said.

Ruda opened one of his bundles and took out the necklace and breastplate. It was everything that he had described it to be. The workmanship was without any flaws, and the gold was pure and heavy.

87

"See how it looks when the sun shines on it!" Ruda said. He held it up for the sun to reflect upon, while a crowd gathered at the rail to witness the spectacle.

But an awful thing happened. The golden necklace and breastplate slipped from his hands and fell into the sea.

There was a moment when no one spoke, and then all together they cried out, "The treasure is lost! It has sunk beneath the water!"

Ruda could not move or make a sound. It seemed that the tragedy was too great for him to bear. Then suddenly his mind began to work swiftly.

"Lend me your knife!" he said to the other trader.

The trader drew his knife from its scabbard and gave it to Ruda. Ruda took it and slashed at the rail of the ship. He carved a large X in the wood. Then, calmly, as though nothing had happened, he returned the knife, expressed his thanks, and went to his quarters to sleep.

The other passengers gathered around and looked with wonder at the mark on the rail, asking each other, "What is the meaning of this thing?"

When at last the ship came to port, the passengers went ashore. As Ruda stood on the beach the other trader came to him and said, "Peace be with you. It was a fine voyage. But I am perplexed. What is the meaning of the mark you carved on the rail of the ship?"

Ruda replied:

"When one meets a difficulty in this life, he must not stand still and ponder. He must act quickly. When my gold necklace and breastplate fell into the water, people around me were shaking their heads, saying, 'Ah, this is fate!' But it was not talk that was needed, but action. You see, in a few weeks I will return home on this ship.

I expect to retrieve the valuable thing I have lost. So I carved the mark on the ship exactly at the point where the treasure fell into the sea. Now, having done that, I will know where to look for it on the return voyage."

The Giraffe Hunters

Masai Tribe, Kenya and Tanganyika

A man named Kume once went hunting for game. He took his weapons and went out to the tall grass. He hunted a long while, and he found a giraffe eating the leaves of an acacia tree. This giraffe was a big one. Many hunters had pursued it but had not been able to catch it.

Kume wanted this giraffe. He went back to the village to get his friend Lumbwa. He told him, "The big giraffe that many men have hunted is out there in the grass. Come back with me. The two of us together will get it."

Lumbwa took his weapons, and the two of them went to the tall grass. But the giraffe was no longer standing under the tree. It had gone to the water hole to drink.

The two hunters made a plan. Kume would climb high into the branches of the tree. When the giraffe returned to eat there again, Kume would leap on its neck and kill it with his knife. Lumbwa would hide in the grass, and when the time came, he would shoot the animal with his bow.

Kume climbed into the tree. Lumbwa hid in the grass with his bow and arrows. They waited. When the sun grew hot, the giraffe came back to stand under the tree. Kume leaped on its neck, shouting at the same time for Lumbwa to shoot.

The giraffe began to run. Lumbwa jumped to his feet and put an arrow in his bow. He saw the giraffe running with Kume clinging to its neck. He began to laugh. When before had anyone ever seen a man riding on a giraffe's neck? He laughed so hard that he could not pull his bowstring. As the giraffe galloped past Lumbwa, Kume shouted, "Shoot! Shoot!" But Lumbwa could not shoot. He was laughing too hard. He laughed until he fell down. He could not stop laughing. He laughed until he became unconscious and lay silently on the ground.

Kume clung to the neck of the galloping giraffe. Then he remembered his knife. He took it from his belt and stabbed the giraffe, so that it fell down and died. He skinned the animal and cut off a small portion of meat; then he walked back to where his friend lay on the ground as though he were dead.

Kume shook Lumbwa, but Lumbwa didn't wake up. So Kume built a fire and cooked a little of the meat, which he put under Lumbwa's nose for him to smell. When the odor of the cooked meat went into Lumbwa's nostrils, he woke up, shouting, "Do not finish the giraffe without me!"

The two hunters went back to the giraffe and cooked a little more of the meat and ate it. Then Kume said, "Now I shall cut up the giraffe, but I won't share it with you because you did not help me kill it. I said, 'Shoot! Shoot!' But you did not shoot. You only fainted. Therefore you don't deserve a share."

Hearing this, Lumbwa got up from where he sat and

went back to the village. There he met Kume's wife. She asked him, "Have you seen my husband?"

Lumbwa answered, "Yes, I saw him. He is hunting. I hear he is very angry with you. He intends to beat you when he returns."

Kume's wife considered this. She thought it would be wise for her to stay with friends until Kume's anger had cooled. So she left her house and went away. As soon as she was gone, Lumbwa went into her house. He sat down and waited.

After a while, Kume came with a load of giraffe meat. He went to a small hole at the back of the house and called out to his wife, "Are you there?"

Lumbwa said in a voice like a woman's, "I am here."

"Take this meat," Kume said. "Then I will go back for another load."

He passed the meat through the hole, and Lumbwa said, "I have it."

Kume then went back for more. When he was gone, Lumbwa took the meat and carried it to his own house. Then he returned to Kume's house and waited.

After a while Kume came again, saying, "Are you there?"

Lumbwa said in a voice like a woman's, "I am here."

Kume passed the meat through the hole, and Lumbwa said, "I have it." Kume went out for another load. When he was gone, Lumbwa carried the meat to his own house. Again he came back and waited.

Kume, he came back and forth carrying the meat. Lumbwa, he accepted it each time through the hole in the back of the house and then carried it to his place.

At last Kume said, "I am going for the last time, to get the skin."

This time when Lumbwa went home, he did not return again to Kume's house. He went instead to find Kume's wife, and when he met her, he said, "Your husband is not angry with you any more." So she left her friends and returned to her own house.

Soon Kume came with the skin. He threw it on the ground and asked his wife to bring out his stool so that he might rest. She brought out his stool, and he sat on it. He asked for tobacco, and she brought it. Kume then asked her to go and invite all the neighbors to come at once.

When all the neighbors arrived, Kume asked his wife if the meat was ready.

"The meat?" she said. "What meat are you speaking of?"

"The giraffe meat, what else could I speak of? All the meat, the meat from the giraffe that I killed this morning. The meat that I carried piece by piece and gave you to take care of."

"There is no giraffe meat. There is no meat of any kind," the woman said.

Kume went in. He saw there was no meat. The neighbors saw there was no meat, and they went home.

So it happened. Kume was not willing to share his giraffe with his friend Lumbwa who went hunting with him. Because of that he lost it all.

The Stone Lute
Bemba Tribe, Northern Rhodesia

HERE was a great Chief of the Bemba people. He had a daughter whom many men wished to marry. They came one by one to ask for her, offering large marriage gifts. Some promised herds of cattle to the Chief, some offered cowries, spears, and horses, but the Chief refused them all. He said: "Many men want my daughter, but only one will succeed. Whoever can make me a lute out of stone, he is the one who will have her."

So many men tried to make a lute out of stone, but all failed.

Then one day a man named Kalulu came to the Chief. He said, "I will make the lute of stone. Give me the tools."

The Chief gave him an adze and a chisel, and Kalulu took them and went out of the village. He found a large stone. He struck it several times with his adze, and then he lay down in a shady place and slept.

In the evening he went to the village and told the people he had begun his work. He ate. He talked. He slept. When the day came, he went again out of the village to the place where his stone was. He struck the stone several times with his adze. Then he rested. In the evening he returned to the village. He ate. He talked with the men. They said, "How are you doing with the lute of stone?"

He replied, "It is being made."

Two weeks passed. He came, he went. He sent a message to the Chief, saying, "The lute of stone is finished."

A messenger of the Chief came to him. "Bring the lute to the Chief's house," the messenger said. "The Chief is waiting."

Kalulu said: "I will bring it. But it is heavy. I must have a special carrying pad to put on my head. Send me a carrying pad made of smoke, and I will bring the lute made of stone."

When the Chief heard what was needed, he ordered his servants to make a carrying pad of smoke. They asked, "How shall we make it?"

The Chief said, "Make a fire and use the smoke that comes from it."

They made a fire of wood. Smoke came out. They tried to catch it, but it slipped through their fingers. They said to the Chief, "We have tried, but we cannot catch it."

The Chief came to watch. They put on more wood. More smoke came out. They tried to catch it. Even the Chief tried to catch it. Then the Chief became angry. He said, "Go tell Kalulu he is mad. A carrying pad cannot be made of smoke."

When Kalulu received this message, he went to the house of the Chief. A crowd was gathered there. Kalulu said:

"You sent to tell me I had asked for something impossible. But is it more ridiculous to ask for a carrying pad of smoke than to ask for a lute made of stone? The one is impossible. The other is impossible also."

The people agreed with Kalulu. The Chief said:

"Kalulu, you have spoken only truth. My daughter is yours. Remain here, be my son-in-law and my counselor."

It was done.

Why the Chameleon Shakes His Head
Bemba Tribe, Northern Rhodesia

MBWA the dog and Lufwilima the chameleon, they were friends.

One day man, the hunter, was coming back from killing game, and Imbwa the dog was trotting behind. Lufwilima the chameleon called to him, saying, "Where are you going, and why do you trot this way at the hunter's heels?"

The dog said, "The man and I are partners. We go hunting together. I catch game for him. He kills the animals for meat, and we share together."

The chameleon said, "Is this really so? I did not know that man shared his meat this way."

"It is true," the dog said. "When the food is cooked, each of us takes what he needs."

Imbwa the dog followed the hunter. Lufwilima the chameleon followed the dog. When they arrived at the village, the hunter's wife cooked the meat, and when it was cooked, she put some in a bowl and set it on the ground by her husband. The man took some and put it in his mouth. Then Imbwa the dog trotted up and took some from the bowl. Lufwilima the chameleon said, "It is true, they share together."

Just then the hunter picked up a large stick and hit the dog on the head, making him drop the meat. Imbwa cried out loudly and ran off into the bush.

Lufwilima was shocked and amazed by what he had seen. He went away shaking his head and saying, "*Yangu, yangu, yangu!* It is unbelievable! Why, the dog is his friend, he helps him catch meat! Yet the hunter struck him on the head! Man is no good. He is ungrateful. I will not live near man. I will live in the bush."

It is true: the chameleon lives in the bush and stays

away from man. Whenever he remembers how the hunter struck Imbwa for taking a piece of meat, he moves his head up and down as though to say, "*Yangu, yangu!* It is unbelievable!"

The Hemp Smoker and the Hemp Grower

Mashona Tribe, Southern Rhodesia and Mozambique

N a certain village there was a man who was a hemp smoker. One year there was a drought. The crops did not grow, and there was no hemp for the man to smoke. He longed greatly for it, but there was none to be had.

His eight sons said to their father, "If you wish it to be, we shall go to other places and search for hemp for you."

The father replied, "Yes, go to other places and seek hemp for me so that I may smoke. Take your three sisters with you. If you find a person who will provide me with hemp and if his house is a pleasant one, leave your sisters with him to marry his sons."

The eight young men went out of the village, taking their sisters with them. They searched everywhere for hemp, but there was none to be found. They were discouraged. Then one day they met strangers on the road and said to them, "We are searching for hemp. Our father is in need of it. Wherever will we find it?"

The strangers answered, "We know a man who grows hemp. Come with us." And they took the eight young men and their sisters to the house of a hemp grower.

The young men spoke to the grower, saying, "Our

father said to us, 'Hemp, I have none. Go out in the world and find some for me, as I am in need.' Therefore, if you have hemp, will you not give us some?"

The hemp grower answered, "It is true that I have hemp. If I give you some to take to your father, what are you prepared to give me in return?"

They answered, "Our father has said to us, 'Take your three sisters with you. If you find a man who will give you hemp and if his house is pleasant, leave your three sisters with him as wives for his sons.' We have brought our sisters."

The hemp grower was glad. He killed a goat and fed his guests. He said, "We shall think about the matter."

When the next day came, he filled eight bags with hemp and gave them to the eight sons for their father. He called his own four sons together and said to them, "Return with these young men to their village. Take your two sisters with you. If you find it pleasant where these people live, leave your sisters there as wives for the smoker's sons."

The party then returned to the village of the hemp smoker. He was waiting. His sons said. "Here is the hemp. We left our sisters with the man who provided it. He has sent his own sons with us to see if our house is pleasant."

"It is well," their father said.

In the morning the four sons of the grower said to him, "Indeed, it is pleasant in this place. According to the instructions our father gave us, we shall leave our two sisters with you as wives for two of your sons."

They went away.

Thus the smoker's daughters married sons of the grower, and the grower's daughters married sons of the smoker. The families became friends. The sons and daughters went back and forth between the villages to visit one another. But the grower and the smoker, they each stayed where they were; they never met face to face.

One day the smoker said, "I am old. I have never seen my friend the grower. Take me there to talk with him before I die."

His children agreed. They prepared for the trip and set out. The man's sons went ahead of him to announce his coming. When they arrived at the village, the children of the grower clapped their hands in greeting. The grower asked, "Who is it that is being greeted?"

His sons answered, "It is the father of the girls that were left with us long ago, the father of the young men who came searching for hemp."

The grower said, "I am ashamed to meet him. I accepted his daughters without discussing the matter with him. I sent my own daughters to his house without speaking to him about the affair. We should have met and discussed these questions. Now I am ashamed. Tell him that I am ill."

They went to the smoker and said, "Our father is sick."

The sons of the smoker said, "Our father also is sick. That is why he came, while he is still alive, so that he might meet with your father. Your father is ill, our father is ill. Therefore, they are both ill. Where is the difference?"

The sons of the grower said, "It is true. Enter this house and rest. Tomorrow we shall see how things are."

So the smoker and his sons entered the guest house, and the family of the grower prepared food for them. But just as the food was being brought, there arose a great wailing in the village. The children of the grower cried out, "Father is dead! Father is dead!"

Thereupon, the visitors in the guest house also began to wail. They cried out, "Our father is dead too! He died in a village far from his home!"

The sons of the two fathers discussed the funeral arrangements. When the next day came, the people of the village said to the visitors, "The day is here. Go choose a place where your father may be buried. We shall do the same for our father."

But the sons of the smoker said, "Let us not do it this way, a grave for your father and a grave for our father. They were friends; therefore let them be buried in the same grave."

The sons of the grower answered, "Can such a thing be done? Have people ever before been buried together in the same grave?"

To this the smoker's sons replied:

"You say people are not buried together. This is usually true. But have you ever before heard of a man who went to visit his friend, and when he arrived, they both died in the same village at the same moment? When was this ever seen to happen? The two friends, they died at the same time. Let them be buried together."

They talked this way, back and forth. At last it was agreed that the two fathers should have one grave.

A grave was dug, deep enough for two men. They carried the bodies of the hemp grower and the smoker to the burial place. First they placed the grower in the grave, then, on top, the body of the smoker. They called out, "Bring stones now, so that we may fill up the grave."

But as they were about to put in the stones, the voice of the hemp grower was heard from the grave. He called out, "I am not dead! Do not cover me with stones! Take me out!"

And the voice of the smoker was heard calling out, "I am on top! I want to get out first!"

So the two men came out, and everyone went back to the village. There a feast was prepared, and everyone ate.

Then the hemp grower addressed his sons. He said:

"I did not wish to see the man whose daughters came to us. I was ashamed because we accepted his daughters, yet I had not spoken with him. Therefore, I said I was sick, hoping that he would go away."

The smoker said:

"It is so. Listen to what is true. When a girl is to be taken in marriage, the matter should be discussed with her father. This is the proper way."

In the old days this was not done, but now it is the custom.

The Message from the Moon

Hottentot Tribe, South Africa

LWAYS it has been this way, since the beginning: The moon grows round and flourishes, then it fades and dies. But then it grows and flourishes again. It dies and comes to life again.

It is said that once the moon wished to encourage human beings by sending them a message. She selected the grasshopper for her messenger and instructed him this way:

"Go down to the place where people live and tell them, 'Just as the moon dies each month and comes back to life again, so it shall be with people. You too shall die and come again to life.'"

The grasshopper began his long journey. On the way he met the hare, who asked him, "Where are you going, and why are you so far from home?"

The grasshopper answered, "I am going to the place where people live. I bring them a message from the moon. I shall tell them that as the moon dies and comes back to life, so it will be with them. They too will die and come back to life."

"You are slow, you are an awkward runner," the hare

said. "I shall take the moon's message to people." He left the grasshopper, and running swiftly, he came to the place where people live. He went in the center of the village, calling out, "A messenger has arrived!"

The people gathered around the hare and asked, "What is the message you have for us?"

The hare said, "The moon has sent me to tell you this: Just as she dies and remains dead, so shall people die and remain forever dead."

When the people heard this, they asked, "Is this the way it is going to be?"

And the hare said again, "Yes, why do you question me? The moon said, 'Just as I die and remain dead, so people will die and remain forever dead.'"

Then he returned to the moon to report that he had delivered her message.

"I selected the grasshopper as my messenger," the moon said. "How then did the hare carry my message?"

"The grasshopper was slow and awkward," the hare replied. "Therefore, I took the burden from him. Just as you instructed him, I told people that as the moon dies and remains dead, so men will die and remain forever dead."

The moon grew angry. She said, "This was not the message I gave to grasshopper. I told him, 'Just as the moon dies each month and comes back to life again, so it shall be with people.' You have told them that people shall die and remain dead. The thing that you told them was false!"

With these words, the moon picked up a piece of wood and struck hare on the nose, causing it to split. Ever since that day the hare's nose has looked this way.

But people had listened to the false message that the hare had brought them, and they believed what they were told.

Notes on the Stories

OST of the stories in this book are from Africa south of the Sahara, a vast stretch of country that covers much of the African Continent. In areas adjacent to the Sahara, there is a blending of races and cultures. To the north of the region are Arabs, Berbers, and other Mediterranean peoples; to the south are the Negro Africans. Among the peoples commonly designated as Negroes there are varied racial strains and diverse physical types. And there are, as well, many distinct cultures developed around tribal traditions. Some of the tribes have had a nomadic history, while others have erected cities and have been agriculturalists from ancient times. Great city states and kingdoms once flourished in western and central Africa, and the power of certain rulers extended over wide areas. In East Africa in the Nile Valley, tribal life was built around the institution of herding. And the Pygmies of the Ituri Forest scorned cities, herds, and agriculture alike, lived in temporary camps, and devoted themselves to the pursuit of game.

In some respects the Africa of today is quite changed from what it was a century or half century ago. European influence, both good and bad, has left an indelible mark on the thinking and the techniques of Africans. The efforts to colonize the continent, with all that went along with such efforts, created African attitudes that today are of prime concern in international politics. They also brought physical changes and values of which modern Africans approve. Political states have appeared where a century ago there were tribal groupings and where only a decade ago there were European territorial holdings, colonies, and mandates. Most of those states today are free and, in a political sense, independent. In some places the Africans' right to self-government has not been recognized, and in a few places it is official policy to prevent that development at all costs. But as Africa has changed, so will it continue to change.

Although modern politics and modern technology are in the forefront, much of traditional Africa remains. In the countryside many people live in ignorance that tribal life is doomed. They preserve old arts, old legends, old music, old dances, old ways of doing things, and old ways of expressing human values.

It is there, in the villages, that the accumulated store of tales, legends, and myths is to be found. The oral literature has not perished like so many of the fine traditional arts and skills of only a half century ago. The great wood-carvers and brass casters, and the splendid tradition in which they did their work, are gone. But the storytellers and the bards remain.

This collection samples the folk tales of many African peoples and regions. Omitted, for the sake of unity, are legends, myths, and (with one possible exception) creation stories. It includes tales about men and animals, with animals often acting out what are essentially human dramas. The animal tale is not just an account of the doings of subhuman types; it is, essentially, a convenient framework in which to establish actors and situations with human attributes and meanings. The proverbs with which some animal tales end really apply to people. The humor and motivations of the animals are really human. Many tales that are told in one place as animal stories are told in another place as stories about men.

We have, here, tales about human and animal tricksters, heroes and pseudo heroes, conflicts, and dilemmas. Some tales are stark and border on the cruel, some are slyly humorous or openly funny, and yet others—many of them—deal with philosophical concepts. Human foibles—reflected in animal stories as well as human stories—are favorite targets of the African storyteller. An African proverb says: "The great tree sees far, but it falls loudly." To witness the pompous man brought to earth is as great a pleasure as seeing the just man receive justice.

These tales contain bits of wisdom that have been extracted out of the human experience through the centuries.

THE SONG OF GIMMILE (Gindo Tribe, Mali): Based on a story recorded by Leo Frobenius and published in *Atlantis: Volksmärchen und Volksdichtungen Afrikas*, Jena, Eugen Diederichs, 1921-24. This tale makes the point that a deed once done belongs to history and cannot be retracted. A song is used to dramatize the idea. Singing is employed by Africans as an effective way of complaining or ridiculing, and it is a common recourse of people who have been injured by others. The effectiveness of this social weapon is clearly demonstrated here.

THE CHIEF OF THE GURENSI (Gurensi Tribe, Upper Volta and Ghana): From a narration by Albert Kofi Prempeh. This tale, which depends for its effect on a play upon words, belongs to a category of West African stories that is unusual but far from unknown. Among the Ashanti to the south of the Gurensi, tales of this kind have been recorded. Among them is a story of how Anansi the trickster kills a man named Nothing; at the funeral feast the children are given cakes in consideration for their crying, and from then until now, whenever children are asked why they are crying, they say they are crying for Nothing. A tale from Liberia has a protagonist named Time, who was once rich but became a beggar, and people say that "Time has changed," or "Time isn't what he used to be." This Gurensi story has a close counterpart among the Ashanti. In the Ashanti tale there is a snake named Gold who steals the Sky God's daughter. The Sky God sends people to find the snake, and ever since then people have been looking for Gold.

THREE FAST MEN (Mende Tribe, Ivory Coast): This tale of gross exaggeration is taken from *African Genesis* by Leo Frobenius and Douglas C. Fox, Harrisburg, The Stackpole Company, 1937. The Mende and neighboring peoples have many of these tales of exaggeration and sheer fantasy. While such tales are known in the Middle East, Asia, and Europe, the tradition of "the big old lie" in American Negro folklore could well have come from an original African source.

THE KING OF SEDO (Wolof Tribe, Senegal): From a narration by Sobihas Tore. The professional minstrel among the Wolof people is called a *gewel*, and his lute is known as a *halam*. It is customary for the *gewel* to sing praise songs about chiefs and great men and, in song, to recite the genealogy of kings. The holy man in the story appears to be a wandering Moslem mendicant or *morit*. The Wolof are nominally Moslems, but they have adopted Islamic belief and practice sparingly and selectively.

THE FISHERMAN (Jabo Tribe, Liberia): From *Jabo Proverbs from Liberia* by George Herzog and Charles G. Blooah, published by Oxford University Press, London, 1936 under the auspices of the International African Institute. The last line of this tale, "Every man should be the master of his own profession," is a Jabo proverb, and the story itself is developed around this idea. A person who is a fisherman should not go to a farmer to get advice about matters pertaining to fishing. The explanation of the dove that it is mourning the death of its mother develops out of the dove's call, which the Jabo interpret to mean, "Oh, Mother! Oh, Balo (the mother's name)! Oh! Oh! Oh!"

A SONG FOR THE NEW CHIEF (Ashanti Tribe, Ghana): From a narration by Albert Kofi Prempeh. The irony in this tale is readily apparent. The custom of praising great personages through songs is common to most of Africa. This story is a comment on the custom of praising, the uses to which it can be put, and the unspoken reservations in the minds of the singers.

THE SEARCH: WHO GETS THE CHIEF'S DAUGHTER? (Ashanti Tribe, Ghana): From a narration by Albert Kofi Prempeh. This insoluble riddle tale belongs to a type of story known widely in Africa. In most cases there is no answer that cannot be challenged, and the query on which the tale ends becomes the springboard for discussion and argument among the listeners. The Mmoatia are not pygmies but tiny supernatural creatures in the folklore of the Ashanti, comparable in some respects to the fairy-like beings in Irish lore.

THE KING'S DRUM (Ashanti Tribe, Ghana): Based on a rendition by S. E. Adu, of Agogo, Ghana. Anansi or Kwaku Anansi (sometimes spelled Ananse) is the spider trickster of the Ashanti people of Ghana. He is noted for his mischief, his wish to outwit other creatures, his greed, his cleverness, and, conversely, stupid actions. Usually he comes out on top, though on occasion he is bested by other creatures. He is the personification of clever enterprise, for which he is held in esteem. Anansi is said to be the owner of all tales that are told, a status that he achieved through performing a special service for Nyame, the Sky God. He figures in some stories that tell how certain natural phenomena came to be. He is responsible, for example, for the fact that the moon (in some stories, the sun) is in the sky. While many Anansi stories have a moral point to make, the majority of them simply recount how he bests other animals of the forest.

THE SKY GOD'S DAUGHTER (Ashanti Tribe, Ghana): Based on narrations by S. E. Adu and Albert Kofi Prempeh. In this tale Anansi the spider-trickster outwits himself, a situation that is always enjoyed by the Ashanti. The general situation—discovering a secret or magical name— is found in the folklore of many peoples. It is embellished here, however, by the fact that Anansi wishes to dramatize his announcement in a pompous manner. Usually the king—in this case the king of kings, the Sky God—talks to ordinary people only through an intermediary and thus maintains the dignity of his office. Anansi, thinking to impress the community, tries to say his piece through the talking drum and, this failing, calls upon his friend to say the name of Nyame's daughter. The talking drum imitates human speech by the use (among other things) of rising and falling inflections common to the language and requires an accomplished player—which, apparently, Anansi is not.

THE WEDDING OF THE HAWK (Ewe Tribe, Togo): Based on a version told by S. A. Antor. A similar story among the Ashanti has the buzzard as the main character and explains that when the buzzard tears dead bodies apart, he is looking for the ring. The idea of a ring being a requisite for a marriage ceremony appears to be a European intrusion. In older forms of the tale, one may guess, some other valuable object was probably named.

HOW POVERTY WAS REVEALED TO THE KING OF ADJA (Dahomey): From *Dahomean Narrative, a Cross-Cultural Analysis*, by Melville J. and Francis S. Herskovits, Evanston, Northwestern University Press, 1958. This moving tale, focusing on a theme that occupied ancient philosophers and that found its way into the thought of most of the world's major religions, answers the question in the Dahomean (one is tempted to say the African) way. While it depicts the misery and degradation of poverty sympathetically, it holds that one need not be poverty-stricken to be virtuous. The African listener readily understands that Adjahosu, though a king, became a slave to the old cloth dyer, herself poor, and that he bound himself to this meanest of all possible fates because hunger and misery forced him into it. The effort of the eldest son to repurchase his father is all the evidence one needs that Adjahosu's legal status as a slave or indentured servant was recognized.

THREE SONS OF A CHIEF (Hausa Tribe, Nigeria): From *Hausa Folk-Lore, Customs, Proverbs, Etc.*, by R. S. Rattray, Oxford, The Clarendon Press, 1913. This brief tale belongs to the genre of unanswerable riddle stories, like "The Search: Who Get's The Chief's Daughter?" And it is also related to the tall-tale kind of yarn, which includes "Three Fast Men." Among the Hausa people there is a great tradition of riding skill, and feats of horsemanship and war are extolled in tales and epics. Thus, the test devised by the Chief calls for an exhibition of these arts.

THE BRAVE MAN OF GOLO (Hausa Tribe, Nigeria): This tale is a composite, based upon a version in *West African Folk Tales*, Book 2, by Hugh Vernon-Jackson, University of London Press, Ltd., 1958, and an oral variant. The Vernon-Jackson version came to my attention first. It was taken in northern Nigeria. In discussing it with a Nigerian of Yoruban origin, I found that a similar story was known farther south. The latter seemed to me to exploit the humor to a greater degree, so I chose to combine the two, while in the main retaining the structure of the printed version.

In this tale the chief character, exposed in public as a braggart (and something short of courageous), relinquishes his boast only a little at a time. As long as possible, he maintains that his courage is superior, at the bitter end settling for courage equal to that of other men of his village. The ridicule of the villagers is as fearful an event for him as the encounter in the forest. In African life, public ridicule of an offending person is a powerful force in the community. In extreme cases a ridiculed person may seek relief by leaving his village altogether. An Ashanti story explaining why Anansi the spider lives in the tall grass (or in dark corners of houses) tells that he was publicly ridiculed for some of his deeds and, therefore, sought sanctuary in these places.

THE FEAST (Bamum Tribe, Cameroun): This tale was originally taken down by Rev. Gilbert Schneider, Bamenda Settlement, Southern Cameroons, and is used by the collector's permission. The moral point of the story is evident—that to derive good from a community situation, one must bring good to it; that if people contribute less than they should, the community suffers.

FROG'S WIVES MAKE NDIBA PUDDING (Bakongo Tribe, Republic of the Congo): Told by Joseph Lengo. The theme of the frog who is fearful of going either to one place or the other to eat recalls a Liberian story (also known in Ghana) in which the spider can't go to one village or another to eat because his sons are pulling on him with ropes. There is an Indonesian variant in which a man misses a feast because two are taking place at the same time, and he can't make up his mind which one to go to first. The Liberian story explains how the spider came by his hour-glass shape, while the present Congo tale explains the meaning of the frog's croaking. Plural marriage is not unusual in African tribal life. A rich man may have several wives, and a chief sometimes may have a larger number. For poorer and less distinguished men, however, monogamy is more the rule. The frog's two wives are, in his case, a kind of pomposity, and there is an implicit moral in his fate. *Ndiba* is a pudding made of manioc or tapioca. There are two countries called Republic of the Congo, separated by the Congo River. People of the Bakongo tribe live in both of them.

TWO FRIENDS: HOW THEY PARTED (Bakongo Tribe, Republic of the Congo): Told by A. R. Bolamba. Reference to the natural characteristics of animals as evidence of guilt or innocence is made in many African stories. Here, the monkey cites the chameleon's drowsy appearance as evidence of his having drunk the palm juice, and the chameleon turns the tables by calling attention to the monkey's naturally black hands. An Ashanti story similarly uses the guinea fowl's bald head as evidence that he carries a basket on it and that he is therefore the owner of a certain disputed farm. Drinking from the same bowl, referred to in this tale, is a mark of close friendship; people who have drunk from the same bowl are expected to show special consideration toward each other.

THE HUNTER AND HIS TALKING LEOPARD (Bakongo Tribe, Republic of the Congo): Told by a Congolese seaman, name unknown. This tale is a variant of a story known widely throughout Africa. The plot is familiar elsewhere as well, including Southeast Asia and the

Americas. In one African version the talking object is a skull, in another a tortoise. The tortoise variant, in New World dress, appears also in Haiti, with a lizard sometimes substituting as the talking animal.

THE PAST AND THE FUTURE (Mbaka Tribe, Angola): From *Folk-Tales of Angola* by Heli Chatelain, Boston and New York, G. E. Stechert & Co. (for the American Folk-Lore Society), 1894. This brief tale belongs to a category of moral and philosophical stories found over a large part of the African continent. It comes very close to being an elaborated proverb, and, like many such tales, has the quality of what we think of as poetry, as well as philosophical or abstract thinking.

THE ELEPHANT HUNTERS (Mbaka Tribe, Angola): From *Folk-Tales of Angola* by Heli Chatelain, Boston and New York, G. E. Stechert & Co. (for the American Folk-Lore Society), 1894. As given in the original, the story is associated with a proverb that says: "They quarreled in the bush; witnesses, we get them from their tongues." The idea is that when two people argue over an incident to which there are no witnesses, it is difficult to render justice, but their own words and actions can reveal the truth. The judgment given by the headman here is spelled out in a little more detail than in the original to make its logic more evident.

A FATHER-IN-LAW AND HIS SON-IN-LAW (Loanda Dialect, Angola): From *Folk-Tales of Angola* by Heli Chatelain, Boston and New York, G. E. Stechert & Co. (for the American Folk-Lore Society), 1894. As is evident from many of the tales in this collection, Africans are prompt to adjudicate differences that cannot be settled directly. Not only lawsuits are handled in this way but also personal grievances that are outside of law. In Liberia there is a proverb that says: "If trouble lasts, it will involve many people." In tribal life, it is in the interest of the entire community that people should resolve their differences quickly, resorting to third parties as judges if necessary. Older people are usually called upon to listen to the arguments and judge. Sometimes it will be a headman or local chief who judges the dispute. Where the problem is not serious, a trusted elder of the community (in this case a group of elders) is selected.

THE DONKEYS ASK FOR JUSTICE (Ethiopia): Based on a tale told by Gherenchiel Hurogo. The story rationalizes two things about the donkey—its insistence on stopping and nuzzling another donkey on the road, and the way it twists its upper lip, exposing its teeth. At the same time, it expresses sympathy with the animal's hard lot.

THE LION'S SHARE (Somalia): Told by Abdul Mahamed Rehman of Hargeisa. This brief tale with its instructive theme has the character of a classical fable and some of the flavor of Middle-Eastern lore.

NAWASI GOES TO WAR (Somalia): Told by Abdell Mahamed. This tale, which seems to be popular among the Somali, is a comic reflection on the reluctant warrior. The protagonist, Nawasi, may be Banawasi or Abu Nuwas, the human trickster hero known throughout a large part of the Middle East. If so, this episode is one of the few in which he almost completely loses control of his situation. Another version of the story is to be found in Courlander and Leslau, *The Fire on the Mountain,* Holt, Rinehart and Winston, 1950, under the title, "The Battle of Eghal Shillet."

RUDA, THE QUICK THINKER (Sudan): Taken from a Sudanese informant at Khartoum. Sudan, with its many tribes of Sudanic, Bantu, and Nilotic stock, has been strongly influenced, particularly in the north, by Islamic culture. Middle Eastern influence is noteworthy throughout a large region of Africa to the south and southwest of the Arabian peninsula—Sudan, Eritrea, Ethiopia, and Somalia. Thus, among other things, one finds stories in common currency that are known in the Middle East itself, or even farther afield. When one considers that the Islamic culture spreads across North Africa, through the Middle East, South Asia, and Southeast Asia into some of the Pacific islands, it will not seem strange that similar stories are told in Islamic Africa and in the Far East. Variants of this particular story, for example, are known in Indonesia, Arabia, and elsewhere, where the character of the self-satisfied trader and the idiocy of his solution are equally appreciated.

THE GIRAFFE HUNTERS (Masai Tribe, Kenya and Tanganyika): From a tale in *The Masai, Their Language and Folklore* by A. C. Hollis, Oxford, The Clarendon Press, 1905. The present version is a rewrite of the original; minor liberties have been taken with details, but the story is faithful in the main to Hollis's presentation. Omitted is the hunter's final solution—to beat his wife for

the fiasco. The names of the two men are an addition to
the Hollis version for the purpose of easily identifying
them. It is not clear in the original whether a moral is intended by the denouement or whether the tale merely
tells how a shrewd trickster outwitted his companion.

THE STONE LUTE (Bemba Tribe, Northern Rhodesia):
From a rendition by Oliver Kabungo. This story belongs
to a world-wide type of tale in which an impossible task
or event is put to ridicule by the analogy of another impossible task or event. Thus, in an Ethiopian tale, the
leopard claims the jackal's calf by asserting his own bull
gave birth to it. The baboon is called upon to judge the
dispute. He sits on a rock and plucks at a stone. The leopard asks him to get on with the case, to which the
baboon replies that it is his custom to play a tune on his
stone before rendering a judgment. "Music cannot come
from a stone," the leopard says, to which the baboon
answers: "And can a bull give birth to a calf?" Similar
tales are known elsewhere in Asia, Europe, and America.

WHY THE CHAMELEON SHAKES HIS HEAD (Bemba
Tribe, Northern Rhodesia): From a narration by Oliver
Kabungo. In many parts of Africa the dog is used for
hunting; yet he is rarely regarded as a pet. Often he lurks
around the fringes of the village, searching for scraps to
eat or bones to gnaw on. Usually he is lean and hungry
looking. Although this relationship between man and dog
is taken for granted, this tale, like many others, raises the
question of why man is so selfish and ungrateful. In a
number of African stories (which have counterparts in

Asia and Europe), man is judged by various animals, trees, and other elements of nature and found wanting.

THE HEMP SMOKER AND THE HEMP GROWER (Mashona Tribe, Southern Rhodesia and Mozambique): Based on a story in *Fables of the Veld,* by F. W. T. Posselt, Oxford, Clarendon Press, 1929. In this tale, the incident of two men pretending to be dead recalls a host of African tales known from the west coast to Ethiopia in the east (as well as comparable tales in European and Asian tradition). In a Somali story in this collection, for example, a timid warrior lies down in his house and pretends to be dead until he is sure the battle is over. In an Ethiopian tale, a man is warned that if he is not careful, he will fall from a tree and be killed; he then falls and, remembering the warning, decides that he must be dead. In Ghana, an Ashanti story tells how Anansi the spider pretends to be dead in order to eat freely during a famine.

In this tale about the grower and the smoker, the two friends' pretense of death provides a seriocomic situation that helps to formulate a moral—or, strictly speaking, a guide to human behavior. In most African tribal societies, it is customary for the father of a suitor, or a designated elder, or sometimes the suitor himself, to approach the father of the girl wanted in marriage. This amenity is especially meaningful in African tribal life, for the concept of family is strong, and marriages produce larger extended families. The institution of "marriage settlement" is also involved—the payment by the groom or his family to the family of the bride, sometimes made in money, sometimes in cattle, blankets, or other valued articles. This does not constitute a "sale" of the girl, con-

trary to much that has been written; it is a guarantee of
the girl's good behavior and a bond between the families.
Should the girl leave her husband without good reason,
for example, her family would have to repay the marriage
settlement. The institution is thus one that consolidates
kin groups and helps to stabilize marriage relationships.
Other social institutions and customs control the behavior
of the husband.

While one is led to deduce from much that has been
written, and from the folklore itself, that girls are given
away or sold by their fathers on whim or impulse, the real
picture is something else again. A discussion between
families on such a matter as marriage may be a studied,
drawn-out affair, with plenty of time for consideration by
all parties. Often the boy and girl directly involved have
known each other for some time and may be the insti-
gators of the discussions and negotiations. In circum-
stances of this kind, there may be a certain amount of
pretense in the discussions, the result being a foregone
conclusion. If a girl is dead set against marrying a certain
suitor, she probably is not compelled. As is apparent even
in the folklore, considerable thought is given to the
characters of the boy and girl and the chances of a last-
ing marriage. Neither family wants a marriage that will
not be stable and, presumably, reasonably happy. In
modern times, even in tribal areas, Christian and Moslem
marriage customs are often followed.

In this story, the moral comes almost as an afterthought.
It is well understood by African listeners that appropriate
discussions have not taken place between the families of
the smoker and the grower.

THE MESSAGE FROM THE MOON (Hottentot Tribe, South Africa): From W. H. I. Bleek's *Reynard the Fox in South Africa*, London, Trubner & Co, 1864. This story, slightly revised from the original as Bleek set it down, belongs to a category of tales that tell how certain things came to be—in this case, how it came about that the hare has a split nose. Beyond that, however, it deals with a universal philosophical question that has occupied the minds of all peoples. As the story ends, it states that men believe what the hare told them, but it does not specify whether the message resulted in man's mortality. Another version of the story, known among the Akamba people of Kenya, specifically indicates that it is *because* men believed the wrong message that when they die, they do not live again. Among the Bushmen, neighbors of the Hottentots, it is said that the sun is angered by the resplendent full moon and kills her by cutting off pieces with his knifelike rays. Then the moon slowly regenerates herself and, finally, is cut down again.